What a funny noise!

Andrew Davenport

D0987795

Once upon a time in the Night Garden...

Makka Pakka came to play.

Makka Pakka,
Akka wakka,
Mikka makka moo!

Makka Pakka,
Appa yakka,
Ikka akka ooo!

Hum dum,
Agga pang,
Ing ang ooo!

Makka Pakka,
Akka wakka,
Mikka makka moo!

One day, Makka Pakka
was getting his Og-pog ready.

He packed his sponge,
his soap,
and his Uff-uff.

What else?

Makka Pakka's trumpet!

Makka Pakka loves
his trumpet.

Pwoo-wee-woo-wee-foof!

What a funny
trumpet noise.

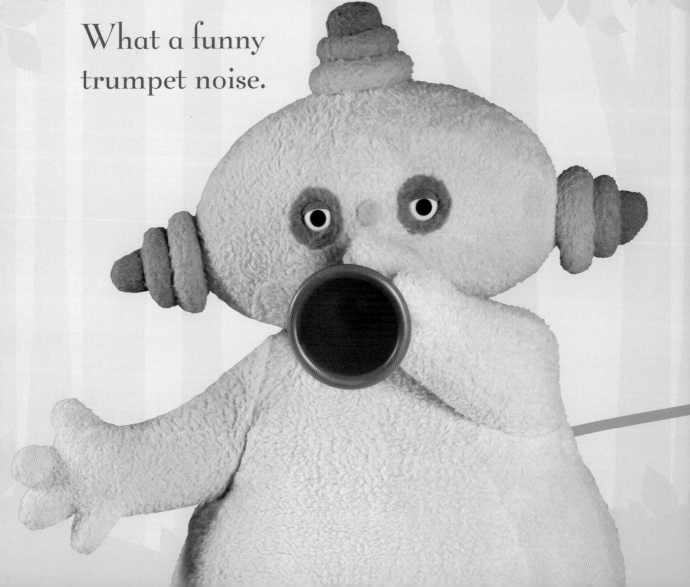

Pwoo-wee-woo-wee-foof!

What a funny
trumpet noise again!

Oh dear.
There is something wrong
with Makka Pakka's trumpet.

Upsy Daisy and Igglepiggle were out for a walk in the garden.

Pwoo-wee-woo-wee-foof!

What a funny noise!

Oooo-ooo!
Upsy Daisy and Igglepiggle
met Makka Pakka.

Pwoo-wee-woo-wee-foof!

What a funny trumpet noise,
Makka Pakka!
What are we going to do?

Pwoo-wee-woo-wee-foof!

Upsy Daisy, are you going to do a dance?

Makka Pakka, are you going to join in?

What fun!

Rattle-rattle-rattle!

Wait a minute.
What's that noise?

Rattle-rattle-rattle!

Something was rattling
inside Makka Pakka's trumpet.

Do you know what it was?

A very pretty stone.

What a funny thing!

Parp-parp!

That's a proper
trumpet sound,
Makka Pakka.

Makka Pakka gave
the pretty stone
to Upsy Daisy
as a present.

Makka Pakka's trumpet
was making a funny noise
because it had a stone in it.

Isn't that a pip?

Once upon a time
in the Night Garden,
there was a funny noise.

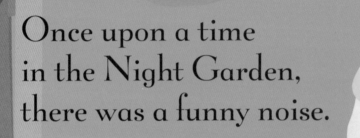

Pwoo-wee-woo-wee-foof!

What a funny noise,
coming from
Makka Pakka's trumpet.

Makka Pakka had a stone
stuck in his trumpet.

Makka Pakka gave
the stone to Upsy Daisy.

Thank you,
Makka Pakka.

Time to go to sleep everybody.

Go to sleep, Makka Pakka.

Go to sleep, Upsy Daisy.

Go to sleep, Pontipines.

Go to sleep, Tombliboos.

Go to sleep, Haahoos.

Go to sleep Ninky Nonk
and go to sleep, Pinky Ponk.

Wait a minute.
Somebody is not in bed!
Who's not in bed?
Igglepiggle is not in bed!

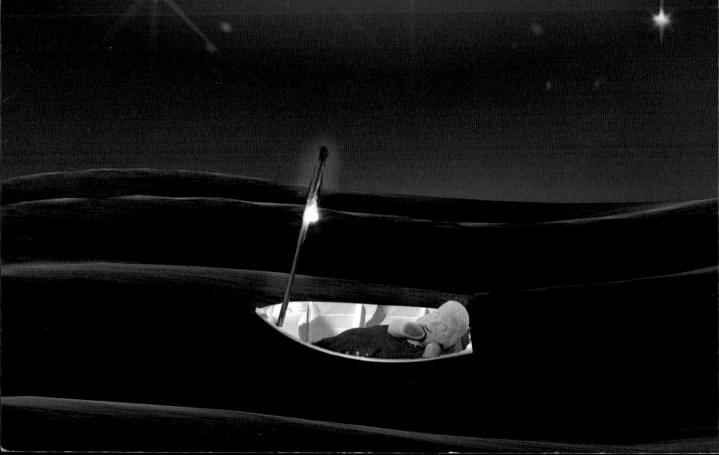